GW00870290

For James & David.
For Ellie, Robbie, Sophie, & Rosie.
For all the children of those who serve.

The majority of the proceeds from this book are donated to the children of service men and women who gave their lives to defend our freedom.

www.mascotbooks.com

I Love You More

For more information, please contact:
Mascot Books
620 Herndon Parkway, Suite 320
Herndon, VA 20170
info@mascotbooks.com

Library of Congress Control Number: 2020923004

CPSIA Code: PRT1220A
ISBN-13: 978-1-64543-778-9

Printed in the United States

I LOVE
YOU
MORE

Written by: Logan Phillips
Illustrated by: Robert Deppa & Kaylee Myers

I love you more
than a smelly
old shoe,

more than a pile of rhinoceros poo,

more than the tune
of a rusty kazoo.

I love you more
than a trip to the zoo,

I love you more than
a canoe of shampoo,

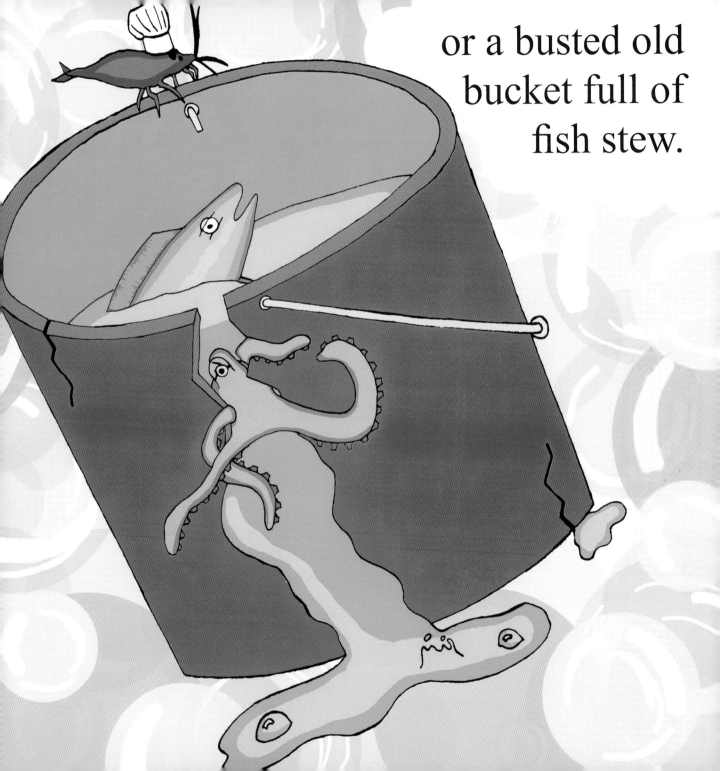

or a busted old bucket full of fish stew.

And I love you more than the ocean is blue,

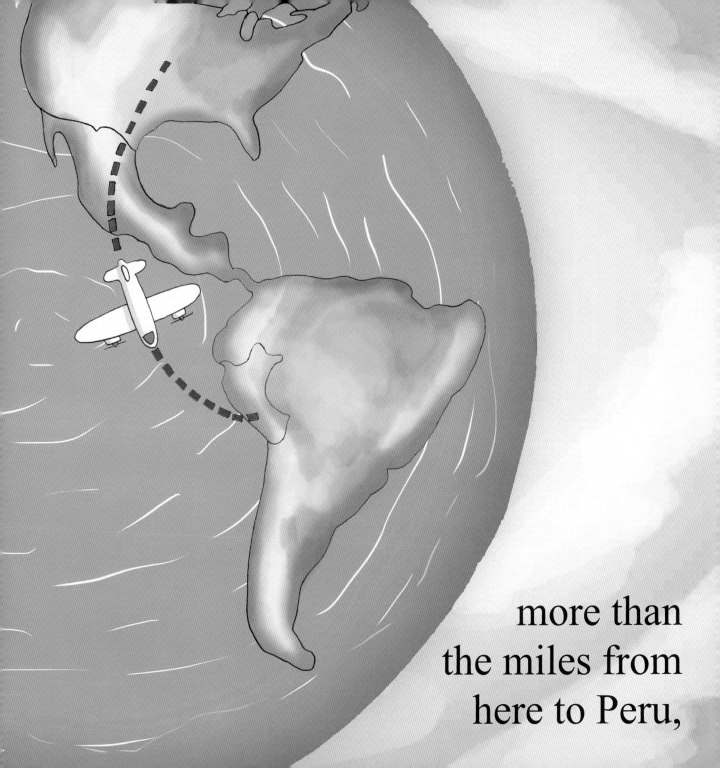

more than
the miles from
here to Peru,

more than the
moon and stars
ever knew.

THAT'S
how much
I love you!"

"Hey Dad..."

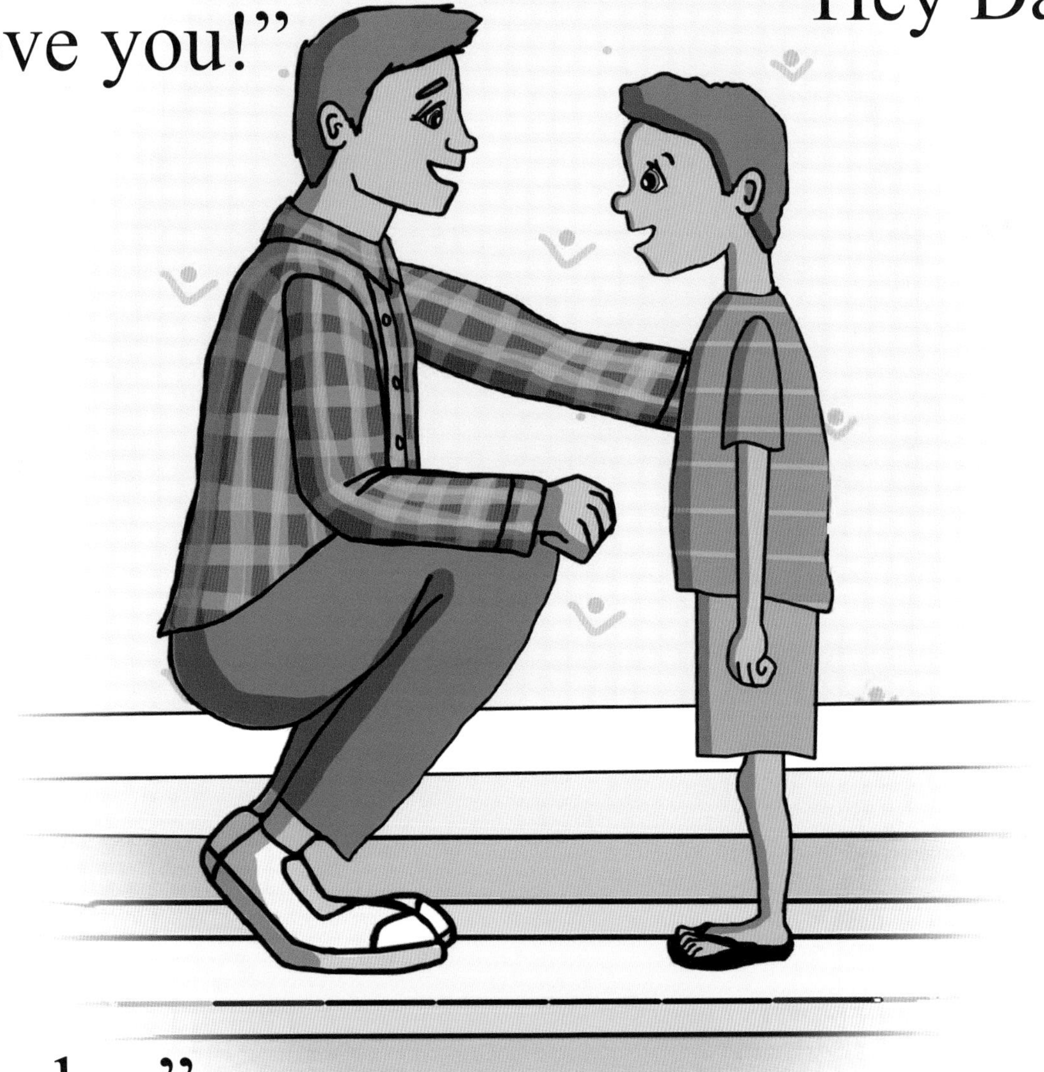

"Yeah..."

"I love you too!"

RESOURCES

The love between a parent and their child is sacred and unbreakable. This is especially true for military members and our first-responder brothers and sisters. When every moment might be the last, we hug just a bit tighter, we laugh a bit louder, and we try to fill every moment with the love to last a lifetime. Sadly, some do not get that full lifetime.

For this reason, we are dedicating the proceeds of this book to "Gold Star Children"—those who have lost a parent to war. Thank you for your love and support.

Interested in giving more? Check out the following charities:

americasgoldstarfamilies.org

theunquietprofessional.org

foldedflagfoundation.org

wegotthisnow.org

gstadventures.org

policeofficersfoundation.org

ABOUT THE AUTHOR

Logan Phillips is like a mushroom—he's a fun-guy! Besides being a dad-joke connoisseur, Logan is a writer, a physicist, and an ardent patriot. But most importantly, he is a devoted husband and father. Having spent his entire life in close connection with the military, Logan also understands the sacrifice of our servicemembers and their families. For this reason, he thinks it is vitally important to cherish every moment with family and fill this special time with laughter and love.

This is Logan's first children's book.

ABOUT THE ILLUSTRATOR

Robert Deppa is a self-taught artist and amateur Bigfoot hunter from the Pacif-ic Northwest. He loves two things above all else: his family and America. He enjoys spending time drawing pictures with his four kids and hearing their silly explanations of them. Although his primary artistic medium is oil on canvas, he decided to co-illustrate this book to share the importance of spending time with your kids and to honor the sacrifices of servicemembers.

ABOUT THE ILLUSTRATOR

Kaylee Myers is a freelance illustrator and Elvis impersonator from Las Vegas, Nevada. Kaylee spends most of her time painting, illustrating, and doing yoga. She has recently joined an art studio and gallery where she plans to teach painting lessons. Kaylee was thrilled to be a part of this project as most of the proceeds will go to the children of fallen service men and women.